Introducing

# The Do'Bees

Angilo EliBee

CurBee

HoniBee

BizyBee

BillyBee

BabyBee

## by WannaBees Media LLC
Be Anything You Want To Bee

In a land far, far away, among the Hive and leaves live some amazing bees called the Do'Bees.

What is so special about the Do'Bees is that they know they can be anything they want to be.

There is CurBee, who wants to be a race car driver.

Racing and race cars are always on his mind.
He cleans and takes care of his cars all of the time.

CurBee goes everywhere pretending there is a race.
As long as he is in his car there is a smile on his face.

Then there is Angilo EliBee, who wants to be rich. He works really hard and saving money is a cinch.

Angilo EliBee would save all of the money that he earned each day, then fly to his honey jar and put it away.

At night Angilo counts all the money he earned, adding and eating cookies as his candle light burns.

He would save and save, putting every penny away, knowing that he would be the richest bee of them all, one day.

There is also HoniBee who wants to be
a famous singer and actress.
She loves to stand in front of the mirror and buzz her
favorite songs over and over and over again.

HoniBee loves to play dress-up and admire herself from afar, she smiles often and pretends that she is a famous movie star.

Sometimes HoniBee and BizyBee put on shows for all the other bees.

Speaking of BizyBee, he wants to dance and sing.
Here he is jamming with his tambourine ring.

Everything BizyBee says has to rhyme and be on time.

Always buzzing around the bigger bees, is BabyBee.
BabyBee is the smallest bee, but a bee you will always see.

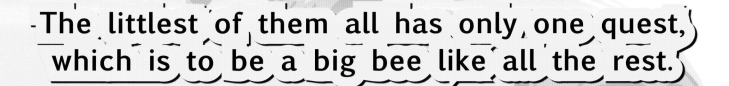

The littlest of them all has only one quest,
which is to be a big bee like all the rest.

Now BabyBee talks real fast, but has great things to say.
She works very hard not to let her size get in her way.

She is always watching, so she can learn,
and has much to offer in return.

BillyBee is the bee that loves to explore.

He messes up, gets back up, and still tries to do more.

BillyBee does not know what he wants to be, but he knows that he can be anything that he wants to be.

He loves to try different things, looking for just the right one, but he never forgets to always have fun.